"S-J, who's that girl over there? She's been staring at you ever since we got here," Timothy whispered.

"At me? What girl?" Sarah-Jane turned around to look.

"That tall, skinny girl with the short, dark brown hair."

But as soon as Sarah-Jane spotted her, the girl quickly looked away and then darted inside the museum door.

"That's weird," said Timothy. "She had this funny look on her face. It was like she recognized you—but she didn't want you to see she was you

sa

THE MYSTERY OF THE
PRINCESS DOLL

Elspeth Campbell Murphy
Illustrated by Chris Wold Dyrud

Chariot Books™
David C. Cook Publishing Co.

A Wise Owl Book
Published by Chariot Books™,
an imprint of David C. Cook Publishing Co.
David C. Cook Publishing Co., Elgin, Illinois 60120
David C. Cook Publishing Co., Weston, Ontario

THE MYSTERY OF THE PRINCESS DOLL
© 1990 by Elspeth Campbell Murphy for text and Chris Wold Dyrud
for illustrations

Cover design by Stephen D. Smith
First printing, 1990
Printed in the United States of America
94 93 92 91   5 4 3

Library of Congress Cataloging-in-Publication Data
Murphy, Elspeth Campbell.
  The mystery of the princess doll / Elspeth Campbell Murphy;
illustrated by Chris Wold Dyrud.
      p. cm.—(Beatitudes mysteries)
  Summary: Their investigation of the disappearance of an old doll
from an antique show helps cousin detectives appreciate the meaning of
the beatitude, "Blessed are those who are persecuted because of
righteousness, for theirs is the Kingdom of Heaven."
  ISBN 1-55513-913-2
  [1. Beatitudes—Fiction. 2. Cousins—Fiction. 3. Mystery and
detective stories.] I. Dyrud, Chris Wold, ill. II. Title.
III. Series: Murphy, Elspeth Campbell. Beatitudes mysteries.
PZ7.M95316Myf   1990
[Fic]—dc20   89-29868
                                                         CIP
                                                         AC

CONTENTS

"Blessed are those who are persecuted because of righteousness, for theirs is the kingdom of heaven."
Matthew 5:10 (NIV)

1
A FAMILY TRADITION

Sarah-Jane could tell that the boys weren't crazy about the idea.

But that was just too bad. It was a family tradition, after all. The cousin whose birthday it was got to decide where their grandparents would take them for a birthday treat.

Well, it was Sarah-Jane's birthday, and she had decided.

"But a *doll museum*?" groaned Timothy.

"So?" replied Sarah-Jane. "On *your* birthday we had to go to a baseball game."

"But a *doll museum*?" groaned Titus. "At least on *my* birthday we went to the zoo."

"Yes," said Sarah-Jane. "But we spent practically the whole time at the oceanarium. We saw the same dolphin show three times."

Titus shrugged. "What can I say? I love dolphins."

Sarah-Jane shrugged. "What can I say? I love dolls. I collect dolls. So I might as well tell you that it's Collectors' Day at the doll museum."

"Collectors' Day?" asked Titus weakly.

"Yes," said Sarah-Jane briskly. "It's Collectors' Day. And they have a special display called 'The Parade of Dolls.' "

Timothy put his head in his hands. "It just gets worse and worse."

Sarah-Jane got out a pamphlet. "This tells all about it. Each collector can bring one doll. It's not like a convention where people can buy and sell dolls. It's just for display. And it's just for fun."

"Fun," muttered Titus.

"Oh, quit complaining," said Sarah-Jane. "It's my birthday, isn't it?"

So Timothy and Titus quit complaining. After all, it *was* Sarah-Jane's birthday. And they had a family tradition to uphold.

8

2
TOP SECRETS

Whenever Timothy and Titus came into Sarah-Jane's room, they pretended that they couldn't believe their eyes.

Titus said, "Why do we have to go to a doll museum at all, S-J? Why don't we just put up a sign on the front lawn? It could say, '*Cooper Doll Museum—IN HERE.*'"

"Very funny," said Sarah-Jane. "But for your information, I don't have that many dolls. Some grown-ups have been collecting dolls for years and years. And they have hundreds. I've only been collecting dolls for two years."

"Yeah," said Timothy. "But at the rate you're going—you know what you should ask for for your birthday next year? A bigger house!"

"Very funny," said Sarah-Jane. "You want to know what I hope I get this year?"

"No," said Timothy.

"No," said Titus.

"OK, I'll tell you," said Sarah-Jane. (There was another family tradition that said birthday presents had to be kept Top Secret. But Sarah-Jane figured that the rule applied only to the people *giving* the presents. She figured it was OK for the person *getting* the presents to tell what she hoped she'd get.)

"Dolls," announced Sarah-Jane.

"Right," said Timothy.

"Like you really need some more," said Titus.

Sarah-Jane ignored them. "Not just any dolls. Princess dolls. There was this beautiful Indian princess doll in the souvenir shop at Misty Pines. Remember? Only I didn't have enough money to buy her. But she had these long, shiny black braids. And loads of colored beads sewn on her dress. So cool! And real leather moccasins, and . . ."

"Why, yes, S-J," said Titus super-politely. "I believe I've heard you mention that doll before." Then he added, "SEVENTY-FIVE MILLION TIMES!"

Sarah-Jane ignored him. "And then the *other* doll was a fairy-tale princess. We saw her in the toy store at Woodhill Mall by Tim's house. Remember? She had long, blonde hair. And a tall, pointy hat with a veil floating down from it. So cool! And this long, floaty, aqua-blue dress, and . . ."

"Why, yes, S-J," said Timothy. "I believe I've heard you mention that doll before, too.

SEVENTY-FIVE MILLION TIMES!''

Sarah-Jane ignored him. "Well, anyway. That's what I hope I get for my birthday."

Timothy and Titus glanced at each other.

"Dream on," said Titus.

"Fat chance," said Timothy.

Then Titus said, "Well, you don't have those dolls now. And there's *no way* you're going to get them. So which doll are you going to take to the museum today?"

"Yeah," said Timothy. "You'd better hurry up and decide."

"Oh, I've already decided that," Sarah-Jane said. "It couldn't be anyone but Princess Emilie."

3
WHO WAS EMILIE?

Sarah-Jane took down Princess Emilie and looked at her fondly. Emilie had been her first collecting-doll instead of a play-with doll.

(Of course, Sarah-Jane still played with her dolls from time to time. Especially when the little girls next door begged her to play Barbies with them. But that was sort of like baby-sitting.)

Even though Princess Emilie looked like a beautiful, little, golden-haired girl, she was actually very old. She was older than Sarah-Jane. She was older than Sarah-Jane's mother. She was almost as old as Sarah-Jane's grandmother. Whenever Sarah-Jane rocked Emilie and stroked her hair, it felt a little strange to think about that.

Princess Emilie was probably not a princess at

all. But a long, long time ago, someone had put a little homemade crown on her head. Sarah-Jane loved princesses. So she thought the crown looked just right.

Emilie had not started out as a princess. And probably her name wasn't even Emilie. But she wore a necklace with a medallion. And on the back of the medallion were tiny, tiny letters. The words were in German, so the Coopers' friend, Mr. Robinson, had translated them. The words said:

For my dear Emilie
From her loving papa
November, 1938

So Sarah-Jane named her doll after the girl who had once owned her so long ago. But who was that girl? Who was Emilie?

The doll had come from Mr. Robinson's antique store. He had brought it back from a buying trip to Europe. And Mr. Cooper had bought the doll for Sarah-Jane's birthday two years ago. Her dad had said with a smile, "For my dear Sarah-Jane. From *her* loving papa."

The doll was in perfect condition. Mr. Robin-

14

son had explained. "I found the doll tucked away in an old trunk, which was almost airtight. So the doll has been very well preserved, as you can see."

In her crisp, blue-and-white-striped dress, the doll did indeed look almost new. And that's what puzzled Sarah-Jane. Why didn't the doll look as though she had been played with? Emilie—the girl—must have loved Emilie—the doll—very much. It was a gift from her father. She had even made a crown to turn her doll into a princess. So why had the doll been put away in a trunk and not played with after that?

Sarah-Jane showed the writing on the back of the medallion to Timothy and Titus. And she told them the story of Emilie—what she knew of it.

"EX-cellent," murmured Titus.

"Neat-O," agreed Timothy.

Suddenly Princess Emilie wasn't just another doll to the boys. She was a Keeper of Secrets.

Sarah-Jane noticed that the clasp on the necklace was broken. She didn't want to risk having it fall off and get lost. So she tucked the necklace away in a drawer. Her father could always fix it later.

Sarah-Jane found herself thinking of Emilie's father, who had loved his little girl so much. But Emilie wouldn't be a little girl anymore. She would be a grown-up lady, probably the same age as Sarah-Jane's grandmother. Did the grown-up Emilie ever think about her long-lost doll?

The three cousins loved mysteries. They even had a detective club. But it seemed to Sarah-Jane that Princess Emilie was a mystery even they couldn't solve.

4

AT THE DOLL MUSEUM

Grandpa went to park the car. Grandma and the cousins went up to the museum. Sarah-Jane had been so eager to get there that they were a little early. They joined the people on the porch, who were even earlier than they were.

Actually, they were at a big, old house. It had only recently been turned into a museum—a whole museum just for dolls.

Across the front of the porch hung a colorful banner that said: *Collectors' Day—Parade of Dolls.*

Already the collectors were chatting among themselves, admiring one another's dolls. Sarah-Jane hugged Princess Emilie and felt very excited and proud.

Grandma ran into an old friend, and right

away they got to talking. That left the cousins free to people-watch. It was one of their favorite things to do.

After a few moments, Timothy leaned over and whispered, "S-J, who's that girl over there? She's been staring at you ever since we got here."

"At me? What girl?" Sarah-Jane turned around to look.

"That tall, skinny girl with the short, dark brown hair," said Timothy.

But as soon as Sarah-Jane spotted her, the

girl quickly looked away. And then, as soon as the museum opened up, the girl darted inside the door.

"That's weird," said Timothy. "She had this funny look on her face. It was like she recognized you. But she couldn't believe it really was you."

"That is weird," agreed Titus. "I mean, if she knows you, why didn't she just come over and say 'hi'? Why did she run off like that? Who is she anyway, S-J?"

But Sarah-Jane just shook her head. "I'll tell you something really weird. I never saw her before in my life."

"Are you sure?" asked Timothy. "I'm positive she recognized you."

But Sarah-Jane just shook her head again. "And I'm positive I didn't recognize her."

The boys didn't know what to make of this. "Tell you what," said Timothy. "Take another look at her as soon as we get inside."

Sarah-Jane agreed. But when they got inside the museum, the mysterious, dark-haired girl was nowhere to be seen.

5
FOOTSTEPS

Whenever Sarah-Jane went someplace new, there was a way she liked to do things. She liked to go all over a place first very quickly. That way she could find out where everything was.

Next, she liked to go back to the beginning where she had started, and go through the place again. This time she would go very, very slowly. Looking closely at everything. Not wanting to miss anything.

It was different when she went back to a place she'd already been before. By that time, she had her favorite spots all picked out. Then she would go right to them and stay there.

Sarah-Jane knew that her way of going to museums drove people crazy. But she couldn't help it. Besides, it was her birthday.

Sarah-Jane had never been to this new doll museum before. So, of course, she was itching to do her "once-over-lightly."

Grandma was still chatting with her friend. But she turned to the cousins and said, "I can't imagine what's keeping your grandfather. Probably got to talking with somebody. I never saw such a person for talking."

The cousins looked at one another and smiled. Both grandparents were great talkers.

While they were waiting, they filled out their name tags. Timothy, Titus, and Grandma got blue tags that said *Guest*. Sarah-Jane got to wear a red tag that said *Collector*.

The other collectors were lining up to register their dolls for the special display.

Sarah-Jane felt torn between wanting to do two different things. On the one hand, she wanted to line up with the other collectors. On the other hand, she wanted to see the museum.

The line was long, and that helped Sarah-Jane decide. She would go quickly through the museum first and then come back to register Princess Emilie.

Grandma said that Sarah-Jane could go ahead if she wanted, and that she would wait there for Grandpa.

The boys said they would go with Sarah-Jane. They didn't argue when Sarah-Jane said she wanted to start on the third floor and quickly work her way down again. (Once they had accepted the fact that they had to go through a doll museum, they didn't care how they did it.)

It felt special to be on the top floor all by themselves. In the glass cases, dolls sat in motionless rocking chairs. Or they sat around a toy table, holding a silent tea party. It was all very quiet and peaceful. From far below they could hear the babble of happy voices as people talked about their doll collections.

Sarah-Jane looked down at Emilie and felt another surge of love and pride. "You are my own sweet baby princess," she whispered. "And I will keep you forever."

"What was that?" asked Timothy suddenly.

"Nothing," said Sarah-Jane, feeling a little embarrassed that she might have been overheard.

"No," insisted Timothy. "Listen. Foot-steps."

They listened. Soft footsteps came down the hall and stopped outside the room where the cousins stood frozen. Then the footsteps moved off down the hall to another room.

"Maybe it's Grandma looking for us," suggested Titus. But he didn't sound like he believed his own suggestion.

"No," said Timothy. "These footsteps sounded—I don't know—kind of 'sneaky.' Grandma would never sneak up on us."

"Let's go back downstairs," said Sarah-Jane firmly.

"Are you sure?" asked Titus. "I thought you wanted to case the joint."

"We can do that later," Sarah-Jane replied. "I want to register my doll. I want to see if Grandpa's here yet."

But Sarah-Jane's cousins knew her too well for that.

Timothy said, "Listen, S-J. I'm sorry I made such a big deal about the footsteps. There's nothing to be scared of. It's probably just some early bird who likes to do museums the way you do." But he didn't sound like he believed his own suggestion.

The top floor of the museum no longer seemed quiet and peaceful. Since the footsteps, it seemed quiet and creepy.

"I can't explain it exactly," Sarah-Jane said softly. "But I get the feeling we're being followed."

6
THAT GIRL AGAIN

"I don't get it," said Titus, as they hurried along the hall. (In the opposite direction from where the footsteps had gone.) "Who would be following us?"

"Yeah, S-J," said Timothy. "It doesn't make any sense. Aren't you being a little jumpy?"

But Sarah-Jane noticed that she had to run to keep up with them.

She could have sworn she heard footsteps again behind her. But when she made herself turn and look, there was no one there.

When they got downstairs, though, Sarah-Jane felt a little silly. The front hall was crowded and noisy. Everything was perfectly normal.

"Grandpa's out helping someone who has car trouble," their grandmother told them.

"Honestly. I never saw such a person for helping."

The cousins looked at one another and smiled. Both grandparents were great helpers.

Sarah-Jane took her doll to the registration table.

"Name of collector?" asked the museum volunteer pleasantly.

"Sarah-Jane Cooper."

The volunteer wrote it in the book. "Name of doll?"

"Princess Emilie—with an *i e* on the end. She's German."

"This is a beautiful doll," remarked the volunteer as she took Emilie from Sarah-Jane. "And what a good idea to add the little crown."

"Thank you," said Sarah-Jane. "But Emilie's other owner made the crown a long time ago."

The volunteer found just the right spot for Sarah-Jane's doll on the display shelf with the others.

Sarah-Jane stepped back to admire Princess Emilie and bumped smack into somebody.

"Oh, excuse me," said Sarah-Jane, turning around.

And she saw that it was the tall, dark-haired girl.

And then Sarah-Jane saw, to her amazement, that the girl had tears in her eyes.

"Did I hurt you that bad?" she asked, wondering how she could have. "I—I'm sorry."

But the girl just shook her head. She opened her mouth as if she desperately wanted to say something. But she quickly seemed to change her mind for she turned and hurried away.

"What was that all about?" asked Titus, coming up to Sarah-Jane.

"It was that girl again, wasn't it?" asked Timothy.

"Lisa Miller," said Sarah-Jane thoughtfully. Timothy asked, "You mean you found out that you know her after all?"

"No," said Sarah-Jane. "But I got a good look at her name tag."

"Red or blue?" asked Titus.

"Blue," replied Sarah-Jane. "That means she's not a collector."

"Good detective work, S-J!" said Titus.

"Yeah, this is great!" agreed Timothy. "Let's do some more."

But none of them could figure out what they needed to detect. So they went to join their grandmother in the first room of dolls. But as they left the collectors' display, all three of them couldn't help turning to take one more look at the beautiful Princess Emilie.

Grandpa joined them a little while later.

"Grandpa!" cried Sarah-Jane. "Come see how great my doll looks in the display!"

"Yes, Grandpa, S-J's is the best!" said Timothy loyally.

"The best!" agreed Titus. "That Emilie doll has all these secrets and everything."

Sarah-Jane thought she was going to burst with happiness.

But when they arrived back at the display area, Princess Emilie was gone.

7

TOO MANY SARAH-JANE COOPERS

Sarah-Jane rushed over to the volunteer. It was a different lady this time, one who didn't remember her from before.

Sarah-Jane could hardly get the words out over the lump in her throat. She pointed to the empty space. "Where's my doll? Did somebody move her?"

"Why, no," said the volunteer, sounding very surprised. "The owner came and got her just a little while ago. She said she had to leave early, because her grandmother was coming to pick her up."

"The *owner*?!" cried Sarah-Jane. "But—but *I'm* the owner!"

"Oh, dear!" said the lady. By this time, she looked more than surprised. She looked flab-

bergasted. But she seemed to be trying very hard to keep calm. "Well, now—let me just check the book. Yes—here it is. The doll's name is Princess Emilie."

"Yes, yes!" cried Sarah-Jane, nodding her head vigorously.

"And the name of the girl who picked her up—yes, here it is: Sarah-Jane Cooper."

"No, no!" cried Sarah-Jane, shaking her head. "*I'm* Sarah-Jane Cooper!"

"She *is*!" said Timothy and Titus together. "We're her cousins, so we ought to know."

Grandpa rested his hands on Sarah-Jane's shoulders to calm her down. But nothing could help the panicky, empty feeling that was swallowing her up inside.

"There must be some mistake," Grandpa said to the volunteer. "We seem to have too many Sarah-Jane Coopers. I can vouch for my granddaughter here. I have no idea who the other child is."

"What did she look like?" Timothy asked the lady.

The volunteer gathered her thoughts. "Well, let's see. Tall for her age, I should think. A little on the thin side. Short, dark hair..."

Titus interrupted. "That's not Sarah-Jane Cooper! That's Lisa Miller!"

Grandma and Grandpa stared at him. "Who is Lisa Miller?"

"She's this girl who kept staring at Sarah-Jane all the time. And—" He paused as a new thought struck him. "And we think she was the one who was following us around."

The volunteer looked terribly confused. "But if this child is Lisa somebody, why was she wearing a collector's name tag that said *Sarah-Jane Cooper*? And if she's not the owner, how did she know the doll's name is Princess Emilie?"

Sarah-Jane said slowly, "She must have overheard me when I registered. She was standing right behind me. I even backed into her."

"An impostor with a phony name tag," said Timothy.

"Smart," said Titus. "Rotten. But very smart."

The volunteer said, "Forgive me, but why steal *this* doll out of all the others? It's lovely, of course," she added quickly when she saw the look on Sarah-Jane's face. "What I mean is, there are several other dolls that are more—um, noticeable."

"I don't know," said Sarah-Jane miserably. "All I know is that my beautiful princess is lost."

"Maybe not," said Timothy. "Lisa was going to wait for her grandmother. And we all know that grandmothers are sometimes late."

"Meaning..." said Titus, before Grandma

could say anything. "Meaning that Lisa and Emilie might still be around here someplace. Waiting. And hiding, I bet."

"Well, what are *we* waiting for?" said Sarah-Jane. "We're detectives, aren't we? Let's go find them!"

8
A SEARCH FOR A PRINCESS

Before they started to search, the detective-cousins stopped to think things through. Where would Lisa go? Someplace away from the crowds. Someplace where she could watch for her grandmother's car.

It was chilly, so the grown-ups were sure that Lisa must still be in the museum. But the cousins were sure she had gone outside. That's what they would have done.

There was no mud to show footprints, so the cousins and their grandparents just started checking all the places where a kid could hide. Behind the porch posts. Around by the side of the house. In back of the huge oak tree.

Then Sarah-Jane noticed something. On the ground by some evergreen bushes, something

glinted in the sunshine. They all went to take a closer look.

It was a tiny crown.

Sarah-Jane snatched it up and shoved it deep into her pocket.

Grandma knelt down and spoke gently to the bushes. "Lisa," she said. "My name is Mrs. Gordon. I know you're in there. And I know you have my granddaughter's doll. What I don't know is why. Now, please come out and talk to me."

After what seemed like a *long* time, the

branches jiggled. And Lisa crawled out. She took one look at Grandma's kind face and burst into sobs. "I'm sorry! I'm sorry!"

There was a lump under Lisa's coat that Sarah-Jane knew was Emilie. Sarah-Jane wanted to lunge for Emilie and grab her away. But something told her to be quiet and wait. She reached into her pocket and curled her fingers around Emilie's crown.

Grandma managed to get Lisa to stop crying. Then Lisa said all in a rush, "I know I shouldn't have taken Sarah-Jane's doll! But I didn't know what to do! The dolls weren't for sale. And even if they were, I didn't have any money. And—and I thought about asking you just to *give* me the doll. But I didn't know if you would believe me when I told you why I needed it. And if you said no, and if the doll was gone after that—you would know it was me."

"We knew it was you anyway," Titus pointed out.

"Yes," said Timothy sternly. "You can run, but you can't hide. Not from the T.C.D.C."

Lisa stopped sniffling long enough to ask

curiously, "What's a 'teesy-deesy'?"

"It's letters," Sarah-Jane explained.
"Capital T.
Capital C.
Capital D.
Capital C.
It stands for the Three Cousins Detective Club.
And why *did* you want my doll so much?"

Lisa took a deep breath. Her eyes pleaded with Sarah-Jane to understand. "Well, see—it's not exactly your doll. I mean—it *is*. But it didn't use to be. The doll's name is really Gretchen. And she used to belong to a girl named Emilie. Except Emilie isn't a kid anymore. She's my grandmother."

9
THE STORY OF EMILIE

The boys looked like they didn't believe a word of it. But Sarah-Jane wasn't so sure. She turned back to Lisa and said, "So—when Tim saw you staring at me . . . it wasn't *me* you recognized. It was Emilie—Gretchen, my—the—doll."

Lisa nodded. "My grandmother told me the story of Gretchen—Emilie, her—your doll. Then I made her tell it to me lots of times after that."

Sarah-Jane nodded. That's the way it was with family stories.

Lisa said, "So I knew exactly what Gretchen looked like. Blonde hair. A blue-and-white-striped dress. And especially the little princess crown my grandmother had made for her. When I saw the doll you were holding, I couldn't believe my eyes! So I followed you around just to make sure. And then, when I heard you tell the lady that the doll's name was Emilie and that she was German . . . well, that's when I was positive. And all I could think about was getting ahold of her so I could give her back to my grandmother."

Grandma said gently, "Lisa, why was that particular doll so important to your grand-mother?"

Lisa swallowed hard. When she spoke again, her voice was hardly above a whisper. "Be-cause—because her father gave her that doll the day before he got killed."

"How did he get killed?" asked Timothy.

"In a car accident?" asked Titus.

But Lisa shook her head. "No," she replied. "The Nazis shot him."

Everyone gasped.

"But *why*?" cried Sarah-Jane. "Why did they do that?"

"Because he was a pastor," explained Lisa. "The Nazis ruled Germany. But not everyone in Germany was a Nazi. My great-grandfather spoke out. He preached that what the Nazis were doing was wrong. And he even helped some people to escape so they wouldn't go to concentration camps."

Sarah-Jane felt a shiver run up and down her back. She looked up at her own grandfather. He was a pastor. And that was exactly the kind of thing he would do.

Lisa said, "My grandmother and her mother and brothers were visiting friends when it happened. They didn't dare go back to their house. Their friends helped them get out of the country. But they had to leave everything behind. And the one thing my grandmother missed most was the beautiful doll her father had given her—her lost princess."

They had all been listening so hard to Lisa's story that they jumped when someone came up behind them. She said, "Lisa, there you are! I've been waiting for you in the car." Then she looked around at all of them with a friendly but perplexed smile. "Why is everyone staring at me? Did I come in on the middle of something?"

Without a word, Lisa unzipped her jacket and pulled out the doll. At the same time, Sarah-Jane held out the little crown.

Lisa's grandmother stared at them in complete amazement. "Gretchen? Is that my *Gretchen*? Lisa, where did you find her?"

Lisa told her grandmother the whole story. And her grandmother told her it was very wrong of her to have taken Sarah-Jane's doll. But Sarah-Jane could tell that Mrs. Miller was overwhelmed at seeing her doll again. If it really *was* her doll. Sarah-Jane wanted to believe it. She did. And she didn't. If only she had some proof.

It seemed as if Mrs. Miller read Sarah-Jane's mind. For she said, "Lisa, we are not *absolutely* sure that this is my Gretchen. My doll had a little medallion around her neck with words on the back." She closed her eyes and said in a faraway voice—first in German, then in English—" 'For my dear Emilie. From her loving papa. November, 1938.' "

Sarah-Jane said softly, "Mrs. Miller, could you and Lisa come over to my house? There's something I have to show you."

Sarah-Jane asked her mother if she could give Princess Emilie to Mrs. Miller and Lisa. And her mother said that was a beautiful idea.

"Cheer up, S-J," said Timothy when he heard she was giving up her favorite doll. "You never know when you might get another princess doll."

"Yep," said Titus. "You never know."

But Sarah-Jane didn't need cheering up. She couldn't remember when she had ever been happier. It was a funny thing. When Princess Emilie (Sarah-Jane would always think of her by that name) had been stolen, Sarah-Jane had felt so empty. But when she *gave* her away, she felt all filled up.

But the story of the girl Emilie and her family

still bothered her. So later she and her cousins asked their grandfather about it.

"It's not fair!" said Sarah-Jane. "Why should Emilie's father get killed for doing something *good*?"

"No, it's not fair," agreed Grandpa. "And we can't understand it all the way. But Jesus said that those who love Him and who do what's right will sometimes have to suffer for it. Certainly Jesus suffered. There can be a lot of evil in the world. And the evil fights the good. But because of what Jesus did, good has already won. Whether people realize it or not. And the happy people are the ones who choose to be on the winning side, God's side.

"Emilie's father chose goodness, even though he knew evil people would hate him for it. But Jesus said, 'Blessed are those who are persecuted because of righteousness, for theirs is the kingdom of heaven.' "

When the time came to open birthday gifts, Timothy and Titus were almost more excited than Sarah-Jane. They bounced up and down

and jabbed each other with their elbows. The way they were carrying on, Sarah-Jane wasn't *too* surprised when she opened her presents and saw . . . an Indian princess doll from Titus's family. And a fairy-tale princess doll from Timothy's.

The dolls were so different, that Sarah-Jane was able to love them both the same. She named the Indian princess "Tiger Lily" after the Indian princess in *Peter Pan*. She named the fairy-tale princess "Briar Rose" after the fairy-tale princess in *Sleeping Beauty*.

The boys were staying for the whole weekend, and that was good. Because Sarah-Jane had a surprise for them. She had already talked to her grandparents about it.

She smiled sweetly at the boys. Then she said, "You know, with all the excitement, we didn't really get to see much of the doll museum. So guess what, gentlemen. We get to go back to-morrow!"

The End

THE TEN COMMANDMENTS MYSTERIES

When Timothy, Titus, and Sarah-Jane, the three cousins, get together the most ordinary events turn into mysteries. So they've formed the T.C.D.C. (That's the Three Cousins Detective Club.)

And while the three cousins are solving mysteries, they're also learning about the Ten Commandments and living God's way.

You'll want to solve all ten mysteries along with Sarah-Jane, Ti, and Tim:

The Mystery of the Laughing Cat—"You shall not steal." *Someone stole rare coins. Can the cousins find the thief?*

The Mystery of the Messed-up Wedding—"You shall not commit adultery." *Can the cousins find the missing wedding ring?*

The Mystery of the Gravestone Riddle—"You shall not murder." *Can the cousins solve a 100-year-old murder case?*

The Mystery of the Carousel Horse—"You shall not covet." *Why does the stranger want an old, wooden horse?*

The Mystery of the Vanishing Present—"Remember the Sabbath day and keep it holy." *Can the cousins figure out who has Grandpa's missing birthday gift?*

The Mystery of the Silver Dolphin—"You shall not give false testimony." *Who's telling the truth—and who's lying?*

The Mystery of the Tattletale Parrot—"You shall not misuse the name of the Lord your God." *What will the beautiful green parrot say next?*

The Mystery of the Second Map—"You shall have no other gods before me." *Can the cousins discover who dropped the strange map?*

The Mystery of the Double Trouble—"Honor your father and your mother." *How could Timothy be in two places at once?*

The Mystery of the Silent Idol—"You shall not make for yourself an idol." *If the idol could speak, what would it tell the cousins?*

Available at your local Christian bookstore.

David C. Cook Publishing Co., Elgin, IL 60120